Eleanor & Mick

"Salt for His Wounds" -- When Eleanor's ex-husband shows up begging for a second chance, she asks her young, gorgeous next door neighbor for a favor and Mick takes advantage of the opportunity.

"The Mercantile" -- Eleanor attributes Mick's detachment to the difference in their ages, but Mick confesses a need for kink. Afraid of losing him, Eleanor reluctantly consents to bondage and pain.

"The Things We Do for Love" -- When her gorgeous girlfriend visits Eleanor on the coast, Mick's obvious attraction troubles her. But, Liz only has eyes for Eleanor.

"Paid in Full" -- Mick's army buddy finds Eleanor hot and makes a deal with Mick. But, if Mick really loved Eleanor would he let another man have sex with her?

"Renovations" -- After Mick spends a month renovating their garage, Eleanor discovers he built in a few surprises.

I.G. Frederick trades words for cash, specializing in erotic fiction and poetry since 2001. Her erotic short stories appear in Hustler Fantasies, Forum, Foreplay, and Desire Presents, as well as electronic, audio, and print anthologies. Her novels receive high praise from readers, critics, and other authors.

A FemDom, Ms. Frederick, owns the man she adores. Although dominant in the rest of his life, he demonstrates his love by serving as her submissive. Ms. Frederick often writes about finding love in BDSM relationships from the authority of one enjoying that for almost a decade.

http://eroticawriter.net/

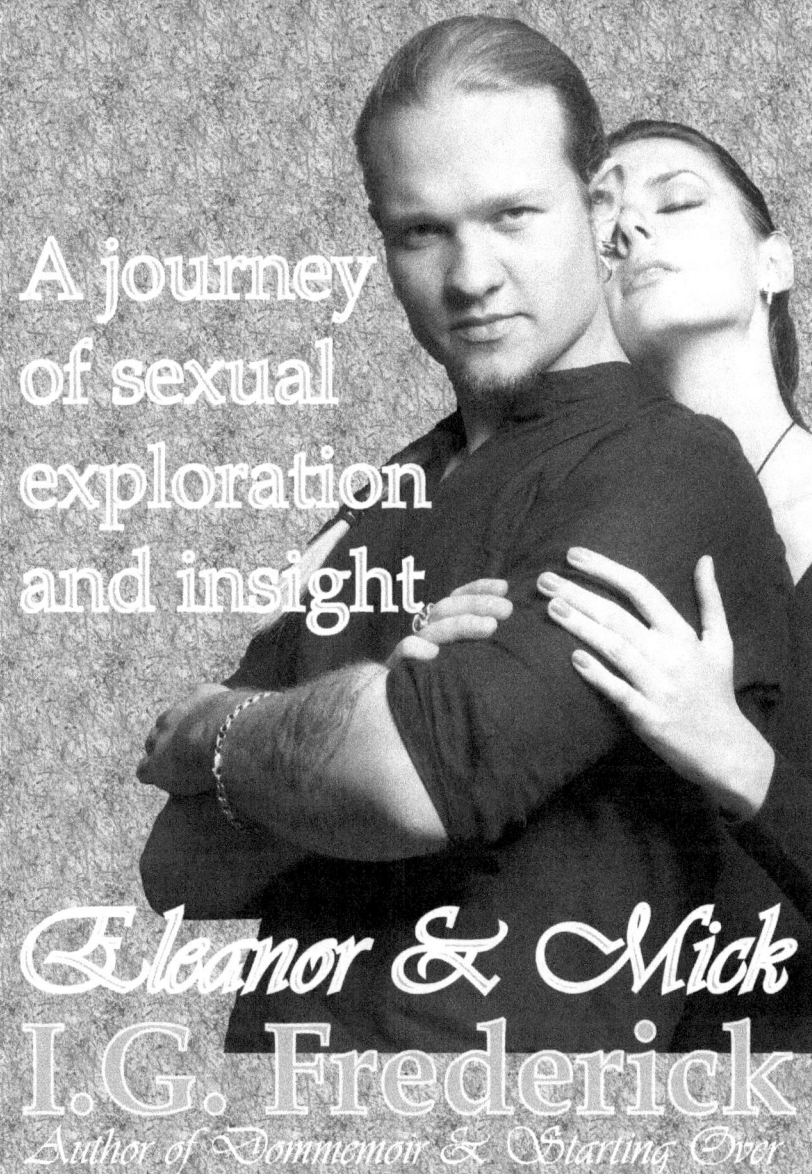

Five steamy short stories

A journey
of sexual
exploration
and insight

Eleanor & Mick

I.G. Frederick

Author of Dommemoir & Starting Over

Eleanor & Mick
© **2014 by I.G. Frederick**

ISBN: 978-1937471-13-2

Pussy Cat Press
http://pussycatpress.com/publisher.html/
P.O. Box 19764
Portland OR 97280

First published electronically in 2011

"Salt for His Wounds," published in Midnight Showcase's
Sweet Revenge anthology, September 2005
"The Mercantile," first published by *Ravenous Romance*, January 2009

Table of Contents

Salt for His Wounds

By I.G. Frederick

I opened the front door and had to hang onto it for support. My ex-husband stood on the porch with a little-boy-lost look on his face that did nothing to enhance his forty-five-year-old features. Geez, he even had flowers in his hands -- red roses, my favorites. Too bad he had never brought me any when we were still married.

"What do you want?" I peered into the soulful brown eyes that used to send shivers down my spine, relieved that I still felt nothing.

He held out the flowers. "Could I come in?" He looked a bit leaner than when we parted for the last time, almost a year ago. His beard showed a little more grey, but the hair fringing his naked scalp was still almost all black.

"No." I ignored the roses.

"Please, Eleanor." His voice whined and grated. "I made

1

a mistake. I'm sorry. Can't we talk?"

"I have nothing I want to talk about with you." My voice was as cold as my heart. I wasn't angry, I didn't hate him; I just didn't care anything about him anymore. I don't know when I stopped loving him. At some point, after fifteen years, I realized I just didn't anymore.

I broke the news to him one rainy Sunday afternoon in January. He didn't take it well. I suggested we get counseling, to try and figure out what went wrong. He didn't entertain that suggestion for even a minute. "If you don't love me, what's the point?" Now here he stood on my porch in the afternoon sun wanting "to talk."

"Look, I know we should have had this conversation a year ago." His voice had lost the grating edge, but it still jolted me out of my memories. "But I was just so hurt when you told me you didn't love me anymore." Well, I suppose he was. But maybe I hurt, too. Maybe I was tired of being taken for granted and endless sexual frustration. "You were the woman I planned to spend the rest of my life with. I reacted badly. Please, Eleanor, give me another chance."

I sighed. "I've moved on with my life, Donald. It's time for you to do the same." I had, too, in a big way. I had packed up everything and left Portland where I'd spent most of my life. Now I lived a hundred and fifty miles away in a tiny little town on the central Oregon coast. I had found a cozy townhouse overlooking the ocean and bought it for cash with my half of the marital assets. I was quite content doing freelance graphic design work from home, making just enough to pay the bills. I didn't miss our high-stress, big-house-in-the-west-hills lifestyle.

"I can't, Eleanor, not without you." A tear crept down his cheek.

"Well, you're going to have to find a way to build a new life for yourself. We're divorced now, remember. I told you if we ended the relationship it would be permanent and complete. I have no room in my life for you now." Living by myself, although lonely, was a definite improvement over what living with Donald had become. I had no interest in going back.

"Look, I understand you don't love me anymore. But surely you miss Portland -- the theater, the restaurants, the excitement? You could move back in with me. We could have our old life back."

Maybe, if he'd suggested this a year ago ... but now I wouldn't consider his offer for even a second. "No, Donald, I don't miss Portland. And, I don't miss you."

He winced. "Have you found someone else?" The pain in his eyes almost made me feel sorry for him. Almost.

"That's none of your business." I hadn't -- you don't meet too many men if the only time you leave the house is to walk on the beach alone or go to the grocery store -- but I wasn't about to let him know that. I thought he would cry and I didn't want to see it. "Go back to Portland, Donald." I closed the door and returned to work.

Engrossed in coding HTML, I forgot about Donald. But about an hour later, when I emerged from my spare-bedroom/office to get a soda, I looked out the window to see he still sat in the corner of the porch, the roses across his knees. *Shit*, I thought. *He's going to start stalking me now.*

I carried my soda back to the office and pondered the situation for a few minutes. Donald had always been stubborn. He truly had been a forever kind of guy. The only way to get him off my porch was to convince him that I had found another man. I picked up the phone and dialed my next-door neighbor's number.

"Mick," I said when he answered. "I need a REALLY big favor." Mick worked out of his home also -- for a high-tech firm in the San Francisco Bay area. His company, and his job, had survived all the cutbacks and the recession. He was probably fifteen years younger than I. We met the day I moved in, although I had seen him before, when I first looked at the place. He had helped me unpack and install my computer and some other electronics. Since then we had become pretty good friends. He fed my cats when I visited my folks in Portland; I took care of his dog when he traveled on business. We often shared meals and even occasionally went up to Newport for an evening out.

Although we seemed to have a lot in common, I knew we would never share more than friendship. The guy was drop-dead gorgeous: green eyes that reminded me of emeralds, thick dark blond hair that swept his shoulders, and a physique that would make any woman wet with desire. His arms and chest rippled with muscles and he had the legs of an athlete. At one time, I had seriously considered drilling a hole through our adjoining walls so I could see what he had inside his shorts. In all our conversations about every topic under the sun, the one I avoided scrupulously was relationships. I didn't want to know anything about his love life.

"What's up?" he asked. His light tone indicated that the interruption was not an imposition. We had, I realized, become a little dependent on each other. I relied on Mick to fix my computer when it went haywire and he occasionally needed me to help him with the numerous PowerPoint slides he had to generate for work. But was this too much to ask?

"See that guy sitting on my porch?" I waited while Mick wandered into his kitchen with his portable phone.

"A suitor?" His tone teased. Mick knew I was divorced, but that was all he knew.

"No, my ex."

"Is he bothering you?" He sounded concerned. "Do you want me to scare him off?" That wouldn't be hard for Mick; he was at least half a foot taller than Donald and much more muscular. Donald was pudgy and not terribly strong. But I knew that physical intimidation would not have the effect of the scheme I had concocted.

"Well, yes and no." I hesitated. I must have lost my senses, asking Mick to do this. He would think I was coming on to him and laugh in my face. I'm not ugly, but I'm not a young beauty anymore either. My auburn hair has several grey streaks and I probably could stand to lose another ten pounds. Giving up my sixty-hour-a-week, high-stress, web design job had allowed me the time to start working out again. I had lost twenty pounds and toned up quite a bit since I left Portland. Mick had converted his one-car garage into a mini-gym -- no health club in our little town -- and let me use it as much as I wanted. Not eating lunch and dinner at restaurants almost every day helped too. Still, I always felt dowdy next to Mick.

"I was wondering if you would be willing to come over here and pretend you're my lover." I rushed the words out before I could change my mind. "I think that's the only thing that's going to convince him to leave and not come back."

The other end of the phone was silent for a long time. At least he wasn't laughing. Probably thinking of a polite way to turn me down.

"Look, forget it," I said, ashamed I had even asked. I could feel the heat on my cheeks and knew my face was beet red. "It was a stupid idea anyway. If I ignore him, he'll go away eventually."

"No, I think you're right." Mick's voice had a funny hitch in it. He probably agreed to go along with me against his better judgment, a true friend. "It's probably the best way to make him realize he has no future with you. I assume that's the message you want to deliver?"

"Yes."

"I'll be there in a few minutes." The phone went dead with a click.

Oh, geez, I thought, what have I done now? I ducked into the bathroom, looked in the mirror, and regretted my impulsive invitation. I wore my standard work clothes of sweats and an old t-shirt. I wanted to change into something sexy, but realized if I did, Donald would likely notice and he might figure out my scheme. Besides, Mick knew what I wore to work. We had lunch together often enough. I didn't want him to think I looked for more than a ruse to get rid of my ex-husband.

When I heard his knock, I went back to the kitchen. Mick stood at the door, gorgeous as ever. Donald, at the far end of the porch, glared at him.

"I decided to take the rest of the afternoon off," he said, as if we hadn't spoken on the phone a minute ago. Mick leaned down, kissed me, and wrapped his arms around my waist. Then he stood up straight so my feet dangled, and walked into the house with me pressed against his chest. He pushed the door closed with his back. My arms had found their way around his neck and my fingers ran through his glorious silky hair. I realized I was breathing heavily and Mick's tongue was in my mouth. I could taste the coffee that he consumed by the gallon.

Mick set me on the kitchen counter but didn't release me. Standing between my legs, he held me tight with one arm while the other hand found its way to my head. He wove his fingers through my hair as he pressed my mouth harder against his. *This boy knew how to pretend.* My eyes were closed, but I looked out through my lashes and saw Donald pressed against the window, a hand on either side of his eyes so he could see inside. *Let's give the man a show.*

I let my hands drift down, enjoying the feel of Mick's muscular back. From this position I could barely reach his ass, but I stretched to grab his cheeks and squeezed. He pressed himself against me and I was surprised to feel he was hard under his denim shorts. *Maybe poor Mick hadn't gotten any for a while.* I wondered if pretending turned him on enough, whether he would settle for me in a pinch.

Mick's mouth had left my lips and drifted down my neck. I let my head fall back, reveling in the silky touch of his tongue. "Wrap your legs around me," he whispered, his breath hot on my sensitive skin. I did, sliding my arms up out of the way and back around his neck. He started toward the bedroom with me attached to his chest. *Oh well, show's over.*

When we reached my bedroom, I reluctantly let my legs slip down Mick's backside and prepared for him to release me. But his lips still traveled up and down my neck and his hand reached under my t-shirt for my breast.

"You can stop pretending now," my voice was hoarse. "Donald can't see us in here."

"Who's pretending?" His voice had that funny hitch in it again.

Mick lifted my shirt over my breasts and buried his face in my rather ample cleavage. His fingers fumbled behind my back with the clasp of my bra. I was panting.

"I don't have any protection." I knew I didn't want him to stop, but I also was afraid his regret afterwards would end our friendship. As much as I wanted Mick to make love to me, I didn't want to lose him as a friend. The lack of birth control would give him an easy out.

With my bra undone, Mick pushed the fabric up so he could reach my nipple with his mouth. He still had one arm around my waist, holding me tight against him, while he fumbled in the pocket of his shorts with the other. His hand came out with a strip of six condoms. If he hadn't been holding me I would have fallen to the floor. This was not a case of physical contact getting out of hand. Men might carry a rubber in their wallets, but they don't run around with a pocket full.

Sensing my knees had given out, Mick picked me up and gently laid me on my bed, pulling my bra and t-shirt over my head. He kicked off his shoes and stretched out beside me, a hand on one breast and his mouth firmly attached to the other. As his tongue rolled my hardening nipple around in his mouth, his other hand played with my hair, his thumb caressing my face and lips. I moaned. At least two years had passed since a man had made love to me -- Donald gave up sex long before we decided to separate. My skin burned everywhere Mick touched me.

I tried to unbutton his shirt, I wanted to feel Mick's skin against mine, but I couldn't get my fingers to work. Mick chuckled and got off the bed. My body cried out in agony for his touch. One by one, he undid the buttons of his shirt and let it fall to the floor. Then he reached for his shorts. He had a wicked glint in his eye as if he knew I enjoyed the show. He unbuttoned the waistband and lowered the zipper so slowly I wanted to scream. Finally he opened it and pushed his shorts and briefs down his hips and legs. His dick jumped out and I reached out my hand, wanting so much just to touch it. As beautiful as the rest of him, it was long and thick with a wonderfully smooth head.

Pushing my hand away, Mick knelt beside the bed and put his mouth back on my breast. Then his lips slid down across my chest and stomach as his hands pulled my sweats and panties out of his mouth's way. I lifted my hips so he could get them off and gasped when his tongue found its way between my legs. He pulled one leg over his shoulder and pushing into my cunt with his tongue, teasing my clitoris, driving me mad. I had three orgasms before he kissed his way back up to my breasts.

He slipped his sheathed cock inside me. Somehow, he had managed to get a rubber on while I was too busy coming to notice. I moaned. He was big and being full felt so good. Mick was probably twice as thick and half again as long as Donald -- who always expected me to put it in for him -- and I could feel the head pushing against my cervix. When Mick was all the way inside me, he stayed there for a minute, letting me get used to the glorious feeling. I wrapped my legs around his waist. Then he pulled back until only the head was inside and thrust it in again, his balls slapping my ass and his pelvis grinding into my clit. I could feel another climax starting to build as Mick slammed into me over and over. This time I screamed. If Donald still waited out on the porch, I'm sure he got an earful to go with the eyeful he had gotten earlier.

I came hard, and my head bounced up and down on the pillow. Mick kept pumping into me and my orgasm wouldn't stop. I just kept coming until I couldn't hold on anymore and my legs and arms slipped back down onto the bed. At that moment, Mick's eyes closed and his lips clamped down on mine as he shot his load. Even with my pussy still pulsing I could feel his cock throbbing inside me. I sucked greedily on his tongue until he collapsed onto me. He still had most of his weight on his forearms, but his chest pressed against mine. He kissed my eyes, my nose, my cheeks, my lips. I looked into those beautiful green eyes and I was amazed at the passion I saw.

Mick stayed on top of me, kissing me, until he started to slip out. Then he grabbed his rubber, pulled it off, tied a knot in the end, and tossed it into the wastebasket on the other side of the room. He lay back down beside me and cradled me in his arms. I waited for him to fall asleep, or get up and get dressed to leave, but he didn't. He just held me, my head on his shoulder, his arms pulling me tight against his side. I didn't want to break the spell, but I had to know.

"What just happened here?"

"That's not a very nice question to ask a man who just made love to you for an hour." Mick smiled. I looked at the clock. I hadn't realized that much time had passed.

"I wasn't referring to your lovemaking. That was wonderful." I lifted my head and kissed him on his lips. I had only intended to give him a grateful smack, but before I knew it I had stretched out across his chest, his arms holding me against him, and our tongues dancing in each other's mouths. Better yet, I could feel him getting hard again between my legs. Donald's idea of a sex life, before he lost interest entirely, was twice a month. I don't think we ever did it more than once in the same day, even when we were first married.

I decided Mick deserved a taste of his own medicine, so I reluctantly pulled my lips from his and let my mouth explore his wonderful, muscular body. I lingered a bit to tease his hardened nipples and was rewarded with a soft, pleasurable sigh. His chest was practically hairless, just a little patch of blond bristles between his nipples and a trace leading down to his pubic hair. By the time I got there, he pointed straight up and I covered his pole and balls with kisses. The sigh was louder this time.

I licked the full length of the shaft, up and down until I had worked my way in a complete circle, careful to over-lap so I wouldn't miss an inch of him, slurping in his sticky sweetness. Then I took the head in my mouth and slowly eased my lips as far down his length as I could go. This time he moaned. Raking my teeth gently along his shaft as I rose up, I paused to nibble the head. Then I started working my mouth up and down his length, tonguing the head on the up stroke. His hips moved with my rhythm and his fingers played with my hair.

He tried to pull my ass up to his face, but I resisted. I've never liked sixty-nine. When I have a face in my pussy I want to lay back and enjoy it. When I've got a dick in my mouth I want to concentrate on pleasing it. With Donald, this was never an issue. I don't think he went down on me more than a dozen times in the fifteen years we were married. I stopped giving him head when I realized he had no intention of re-ciprocating and I had forgotten just how good a mouthful of cock tasted.

The muscles in Mick's legs and ass tightened and he tugged on my hair, trying to get me to stop. "I don't want to come without you," he said through gritted teeth. I spotted the rest of the condoms on the floor and grabbed the strip. Pulling one wrapper open I took out the sheath and rolled it down over Mick's massive cock. Then I positioned my hips over his and lowered myself onto him. We both moaned as the exquisite sensation overwhelmed us. Mick reached up and fondled my breasts. I leaned forward on my arms and began sliding up and down his long pole, rubbing my clit against him in between strokes.

I watched Mick's face. His eyes were partially open, but I could only see the whites. His lips parted and his nostrils flared. He raised and lowered his hips, thrusting up into my down stroke. I could feel my orgasm building, but I didn't want to come yet. The delicious sensation of mounting tension, combined with the glorious hardness of his cock filling my wet pussy, felt too good. I stopped moving for a moment and sat up. I clenched and unclenched my pussy muscles around Mick's cock. A big grin spread across his face and he looked up at me with eyes glazed over by lust.

Releasing my breasts, he sat up and wrapped his arms around me. He started rocking back and forth. Now I rolled my eyes back inside my head. My clit was getting over stimulated and I lost all control. I think this orgasm lasted longer than the one before. When I started coming, Mick slid his legs over the edge of the bed and lifted me up and down on his cock. I was still coming when he exploded inside me. The two of us held onto each other until my throbbing stopped. I couldn't move. Mick laid me back across the bed, got rid of the condom and then took me in his arms again. I would have been perfectly happy to just stay like this forever.

"To answer your question...," Mick paused.

Talk about a delayed reaction.

"I've wanted you from the first day you moved in here. At the time, I thought you might still be getting over your divorce. You didn't talk about it much and I figured maybe you were still kind of raw, so I gave you some time." I managed to get my head off his shoulder long enough to look him in the eye. He was serious. This hunk of a man was attracted to me. How had I missed that?

"Then we started to become friends and, well, you never seemed interested in going any further than that. I was afraid if I made a pass at you and you turned me down you'd be reluctant to continue our friendship." Mick stroked my hair with one hand while the other played with my tit. "You don't know how many times I jacked off pretending I was playing with these." He squeezed my breast.

"Anyway, when you called today, at first I was afraid I couldn't help you. I didn't think I could pretend to be your lover without getting carried away." He leaned over and planted a quick kiss on my nipple. "Then I realized you'd just handed me the perfect opportunity. Worst case scenario, if you weren't interested you'd let me know and I would apologize for getting into my role too much and we'd be able to continue where we left off. But if by any chance you might be attracted to me, this was my one hope of finding out." He shifted slightly and gently pressed his lips to mine for a moment. "I should send your ex-husband a thank you card."

"That would be rubbing salt in his wounds," I scolded. But, I had to admit, I was grateful Donald had showed up. To think, Mick and I been fantasizing about each other all this time. For all I knew, we could have been having mutual orgasms without even realizing it.

I lay in Mick's arms without speaking. I was drifting, almost asleep, when Mick cleared his throat. "Eleanor, I know you haven't seen anyone since you moved here." I looked at him in alarm. Had he been spying on me? "You almost never leave your house except when you walk on the beach and the only visitors I've seen until today were your folks."

I guess we live close enough to know each other's business. I was well aware that he never had women over, but I just figured he went to their places -- and I didn't really want to know anyway. He was right about my social life, though. I had turned into a hermit. He probably was the only person in town with whom I had exchanged more than four words at a time. I settled back onto his shoulder.

"Was this just because you haven't had sex in so long?" He swallowed. "I mean, you never expressed any interest in me before."

I lifted my head once more and looked at him in amazement. I wanted to cry. He looked so vulnerable, as if he had bared his soul to me and was afraid I would slash it open.

"One of the reasons I bought this place is because I liked the scenery," I ran my hand up and down the muscular expanse of his chest, "and I'm not referring to the ocean view." Mick had been working on his truck, naked from the waist up, the day the realtor showed me my townhouse for the first time. Whenever I looked at other places, I couldn't get that picture out of my mind.

"I've had the hots for you from the first moment I saw you, but I always figured I was too old for you. I kept my feelings to myself because I didn't need another rejection." Nothing like having her own husband turn her down to smash a woman's self esteem.

His eyes lit up with delight and all traces of vulnerability disappeared. "You've got to be kidding. Just how young do you think I am?"

"I figure you can't be more than twenty five." My hand still roamed across the muscles of his chest. His breathing was even, but his nipples had hardened again.

"I'm thirty-one, silly." Okay, so he was only nine years younger than me, not fifteen. "The same age as you."

My hand stopped and I looked into his amazing eyes. "Wherever did you get the idea that I was thirty-one?" I suppose I should be flattered, but now I could only worry how he would react to the difference in our ages.

"Aren't you? I mean your hair's a little grey, but being married to an old fuddy-duddy like Donald could do that to you." Mick shifted his weight so he was on his side looking down at me. "You don't have any wrinkles." He traced my eyes and my lips with his fingers. "And you're in great shape. I don't like women who are so skinny their bones press into you when you make love to them." His hand slid down my neck, along my breasts, and across my belly. "Women are supposed to be soft."

I may as well get this over with. It was nice while it lasted. "I'm thirty-nine years old, Mick, I'll be forty in three months."

His expression didn't change; his hand kept wandering, exploring my body with long, soft fingers. "Nope, not a day over thirty-one," he said as if he hadn't heard my confession.

I started to protest, but he covered my mouth with his -- a soft, gentle kiss with only a hint of the passion we had shared such a short while ago. His lips worked their way down my jaw to my neck.

"Aren't we a pair of fools?" His hot breath caressed my skin. A few moments passed before it sank in -- he didn't care one little bit how old I was. His mouth found its way back to my breast and we both started breathing heavily. I tangled my fingers in his silky hair and pulled his face toward mine.

"I guess we'll just have to work harder to make up for lost time," I whispered before our mouths clamped together again.

The Mercantile
By I.G. Frederick

The drip, drip, drip from the bathroom interrupted my dreams. I do so love waking up with Mick's arm across my chest and his head pillowed on my shoulder, but not when the red numbers of the clock have just ticked off one-thirty. I managed to slip out from under his arm without waking him and climbed out of bed. In the bathroom, I closed the door before turning on the light. No matter how tightly I turned the tap, I couldn't get the faucet to stop dripping. In desperation, I crawled under the sink and shut it off at the supply.

"You probably just need new washers." Mick gathered me into his arms when I crawled back into bed. "We can drive over to the Mercantile in the morning and I'll install them as soon as we get back."

I planted a thank you kiss under his ear lobe and tried unsuccessfully to go back to sleep. Since Mick and I had discovered our mutual, long-secret attraction for each other four months ago, we had alternated sleeping at his place and mine--didn't want to upset his dog or my cats with too-long an ab-

17

sence. We teased each other about knocking out the bedroom wall and making our two adjoining townhouses overlooking the beach on the central Oregon coast, into one. But practicality always dissuaded us. If nothing else, we both needed the separation during the workday when I tackled my freelance graphic design business and he created and tested computer security systems for his San Francisco employer.

The last couple of weeks, though, I had sensed a subtle change in his demeanor, a distance between us, especially when we made love. I feared Mick had second thoughts about getting involved with a divorced woman nine years his senior. He probably needed someone his own age with a flat belly and tits that didn't sag.

Brooding kept me awake the rest of the night. I decided to confront him, offer to let him go, and hope that we could remain friends. The thought of returning to my sexless existence cramped my stomach. At least now--I tried to console myself--I would have memories of him instead of just fantasies.

After a quick workout in Mick's garage-turned-gym, we showered in our own bathrooms to save time and make sure we actually got washed and dressed. Then, we climbed into his pickup and headed down the hill to Highway 101. We decided to stop for breakfast at The Joe's before visiting the hardware store. I thought that the café, might be the best place to have the conversation, away from the reality that, whether lovers or not, we lived side-by-side.

After Suzie took our orders and our menus, I looked into Mick's green eyes and hoped I could avoid breaking into tears. "What's her name?" Probably not the most diplomatic way to begin this conversation, but I had to start somewhere.

Mick just stared at me, his head tilted to one side, his eyes wide and questioning. "What *are* you talking about?"

I decided I needed to act less defensive if I wanted to get an answer. "You've been very distant these past couple of weeks. You say nothing's wrong at work. You don't speak to your family. So I can only guess that you've met someone you want to get to know better. I just wondered who." My throat tightening, I sipped the hot coffee without tasting it, still fighting tears.

Mick glanced around the restaurant. Several other locals and a couple of tourists occupied tables. He looked torn, unsure of whether to tell me the truth, I imagined.

I put my hand over his and lowered my voice. "Look, Mick, I understand; I do. I always knew this couldn't last, not with the age difference." *And the difference in our appearances.* Drop-dead gorgeous, Mick has long thick, dark blond hair, a chest rippling with muscles, and the legs of an athlete. I'm ten pounds overweight, I find more grey hairs mixed in with the auburn every day, and the best thing you can say about my brown eyes is that they're not bloodshot.

"I want you to be happy, Mick; I really do. If we can continue to be friends, I'll be okay. I can manage losing you as lover, but I can't stand losing your friendship."

Mick's face got red and I could see a vein throbbing in his forehead. He just glared at me for a moment and then got up from the table and walked over toward the restrooms. He returned just as Suzie set down his three-cheese omelet and my scone and fruit bowl.

"Eleanor, you've got to stop dwelling on the age difference. I can't bear to have you think I'm losing interest every time I get a little moody." His words made no sense. Neither did the look in his eyes. At least the vein had stopped throbbing.

Mick cut off a chunk of his omelet with his fork and blew across the eggs before taking the bite into his mouth. I speared a piece of cantaloupe and chewed on it, but it could have been pineapple or watermelon for all I tasted.

Reaching across the table, he entwined his fingers with mine. "I'm falling in love with you, Eleanor. You're the only woman I want to get to know better." He squeezed my hand.

His touch made my blood quicken and my breathing get ragged. "But, you've been so preoccupied lately, especially..."

Mick pulled my hand close enough that he could kiss my fingertips. The warmth of his touch made it impossible for me to think straight. "Let's enjoy breakfast, Eleanor. We'll talk later."

We didn't, of course. During breakfast, we discussed the headlines, and my folks, and driving up to Portland for the Mt. Hood Jazz Festival, anything but our relationship. In the truck between the restaurant and the Mercantile, Mick only said, "I might want to pick up a few other things at the hardware store." Then, he turned on a satellite radio station so we could listen to the news.

The Mercantile catered to both locals and tourists, so product lines ranged from basic hardware, plumbing supplies, and kitchen items to fishing gear, camping equipment, and souvenirs. Old Barnaby Mekan, the owner, latched onto me as soon as we set foot inside the store. Floor-to-ceiling shelves, crammed with everything from bolt cutters and gallons of paint to crab pots and clam shovels, flanked narrow aisles. Barnaby led me over to the plumbing supplies and found just what he said I needed. The tingle of the bell attached to the front door distracted him, so I set off looking for Mick, replacement washers in hand. I found him standing in front of rolls of twine, rope, and chain links with a pensive look on his face.

"I found the parts for the sink." I touched his arm and he shook his head as if coming out of a reverie. "You need something?"

"Want something," he whispered.

"Why are you whispering?" I kept my voice low as well. My eyes darted back and forth in the aisle, but Barnaby stood in front of the fishing lures on the other side of the store talking to a tourist and I couldn't see anyone else.

Mick reached for the chain on one of the rolls in front of us and pulled out a length of it. He wrapped the inch-long links around my wrist. "Eleanor, have you ever done anything kinky?"

The metal cold against my skin startled me and I stared at him, wide-eyed. "What kind of kinky do you mean?"

"Do you know what BDSM is?"

I swallowed hard and nodded. I knew what the letters stood for. I didn't want to know much more than that, although I had a basic understanding of what it involved.

"Have you ever wanted to try it?"

I closed my eyes. I had never experienced any desire to be tied up or spanked, and never understood why people got aroused by leather and bondage. But if that turned Mick on... Despite his assurances, I knew the age difference would matter eventually. If I refused to let him get kinky with me, I imagined he would look elsewhere. I opened my eyes. "I might be willing to try it with you," I whispered.

He tilted my chin up so he could look into my eyes. I got lost in the emerald green of his gaze and almost didn't hear his response. "I want to chain you to the bed, whip you, and fuck you until you can't take any more."

I slid my arms around Mick's waist and clung to him. My knees felt like rubber and my heart beat faster. I hoped he would think desire, not fear, generated the shiver that ran through me. I have a very low tolerance for pain.

Mick kissed me. "Shall we purchase the necessary equipment?"

"Here?" I pushed my hands against Mick's chest, but he had wrapped his arms around me and easily prevented my escape. "Mick, we can't buy that kind of stuff here," I whispered. "And even if we could, this is such a small town. People would talk." And I needed time to think about what I had agreed to.

Mick laughed. "Actually, we can get everything we need here at the Mercantile, but I promise, no one will know what we're buying the stuff for. You game?"

I nodded, horrified, longing to run from the store. Only the fierce need I had for Mick kept my feet from heading for the door. He had said he was falling in love with me; I had long ago passed that stage. No one else touched me the way he did, physically or mentally. I had thought I had found my soul mate. Now, I wondered.

"Wait here." Mick left me blinking in a vain attempt to regain my equilibrium. He returned moments later, pushing a shopping cart with Barnaby trailing after him.

"I need four lengths of this chain, four feet each." Mick pointed to the links he had fondled.

"That dog giving you trouble?" Barnaby measured out the chain, cut the links, and poured it all into a bag. He wrote the price on the outside with a felt-tipped pen.

Mick took it and dropped it in the cart. "I just want to give her more options."

"Anything else?" Barnaby capped the marker and stuck it back in a shirt pocket already stained with ink from other pens.

"Thanks, we can probably find the rest of what we need ourselves. You can point me toward the safety spring snap rings, though."

"Two aisles over, on the right, near the floor." The bell chiming again, Barnaby turned and headed back toward the front of the store.

Mick pushed the cart in the direction Barnaby had indicated, and I watched while he selected eight rings, dropped them into a bag, and added them to the cart. "Pet supplies next."

I followed him through the aisles, almost bumping into him when he stopped at a display of bandanas hanging off one end of the shelves. Mick selected two red ones. Leaning close to my ear he tossed first one then the other in the cart and whispered, "Blindfold and gag."

My breath came in raspy gasps. I found walking difficult with rubbery knees. *How do I get out of this?*

When Mick found the pet section, he looked up and down the aisles to make sure no one else could see us. He selected a small, red, nylon collar from the ones hanging on the rack and wrapped it around my wrist. He smiled at me when it encircled my arm with room to spare. Squatting at my feet, he tried the collar around my ankle. After making sure it fit, he slid his hand up my shin and thigh and into the leg of my shorts, worming his finger inside the crotch of my panties. Of course, that made me wet. Anytime Mick touched me I got wet, but I think he misinterpreted my desire.

With a wicked a grin that lit up his eyes, Mick stood, brought his hand to his mouth, and sucked the taste of me from his finger. "I'm glad this is turning you on as much as me." He grabbed three more of the collars and threw all four of them into the cart. Pulling me toward him, Mick enfolded me in his arms and kissed the side of my neck. He rubbed his crotch against my hip and I could feel his erection through his loose-fitting denim shorts.

"That just leaves us looking for an appropriate whip substitute. You've never done this, have you?"

I shook my head, unable to speak, torn between the desire his stiff rod engendered and the fear for what he planned to do with the contents of the cart.

"Too bad. If you had, you could tell me if you preferred a cane, whip, flogger, or paddle." Mick ran his fingers through my hair and his lips moved from neck to lips. "Since you've never been whipped, I'll go for something wide to start." Keeping one arm around my waist, the other hand maneuvering the cart, Mick wandered over to the kitchen utensils. After rummaging around for a bit, he selected a plastic icing spreader. He slapped it against his hand and raised one eyebrow above the other. "Want to try it before I buy it?"

I looked around furtively and shook my head. We already had behaved badly enough to get thrown out of the store.

"You sure you're ready for this?" Mick's face scrunched up and his eyes wandered over my face.

I found my voice. "You tasted how ready I am," I lied, fear giving my voice a husky tone.

"And you taste so very good." Mick pulled me closer and

kissed the top of my head. "The first time, I might just tie you up and eat you until you beg for mercy."

I shivered despite the August heat against which the store's intermittent air conditioning couldn't compete. *That* I probably could enjoy. After living for fifteen years with a man who almost never went down on me, Mick's appreciation and capacity for eating pussy never ceased to amaze me. *Another reason to let him experience his fantasy*, I told myself.

Mick grabbed a package of clothes pins and stopped at the paint section on the way toward the front to add a wooden stirrer to the cart.

While Barnaby rang up our purchases, I avoided blushing by thinking about dogs and work and anything else I could bring to mind besides sex. Mick threw the bag in the back of his pickup truck and opened the passenger-side door. Instead of helping me up, as he normally did, with his hands on my waist, he planted his palms firmly against my ass and boosted me into the seat, squeezing my cheeks. Standing in the open door, blocking me from the view of anyone else in the parking lot, he slid one hand up my bare leg, finding his way into my shorts again. Then he leaned down, planted a wet kiss on my thigh, waited until I swung my legs inside, stepped back and closed the door.

I scooted over to the middle of the bench seat, unlocked his door, and fastened the belt around my waist. When Mick got in the truck, I put my hand on his thigh. During the short drive home, I ran my fingers along the inside of one thigh, dragging them across his bulging crotch, and along the other. He squirmed and his erection got bigger. At least I could look forward to enjoying that.

When he parked the truck in front of his garage, Mick asked, "Your place or mine?"

"Well, mine has the dripping faucet. I don't want that to distract us." I really just didn't want to be tied to my own bed.

"Oh, I don't think anything can distract me from you right now." Mick grabbed a fistful of my hair in his fingers, tugged until my head fell back, and nibbled on my neck. "Pick a safe-word."

I thought for a moment. I couldn't imagine sweet, gentle Mick getting so rough that I needed to stop him with a prearranged signal. I would let him do what he wanted, show him I could be everything he needed in a woman. He had worked his way up to my ear and had my lobe in his teeth. His grip on my skin tightened and the pain sent a shock through my system, but he continued to bite harder. I gasped, wondering if he could bite through my earlobe. "Monkeyshines."

Mick sucked softly on my lobe for a moment and then covered my mouth with his own. He thrust his tongue deep inside and I sucked on it eagerly, whimpering when he pulled away. "Once we get inside that door," Mick nodded his head toward his townhouse. "I am the master and you are the slave. The only question is whether you are a willing or unwilling slave."

I didn't hesitate. "Unwilling." At least I could offer something truthful.

Mick chuckled. He opened the door to the truck, grabbed the bag out of the back, and walked toward the door. I took a deep breath and followed. Mick had already disappeared from the kitchen when I closed the door behind me. I heard the rattling of chains in the bedroom and decided to wait until he was ready for me.

I kneeled down to pet Nora, Mick's border collie. A fist in my hair jerked me to my feet and Mick bent my arm behind my back. He pushed me down the hall to the bedroom.

I saw the pet collars, hooked with the snap rings to the chain lengths, at the four corners of the bed. Mick had looped the other end of the chains around the legs of the frame, using the rest of the rings to secure them. He pushed me face down onto the bed, released my hair, and yanked my shorts and panties over my hips and down my legs. Still holding my arm bent behind my back, he slapped my ass with his open palm hard enough to make me jump. Much to my surprise, my pussy got wetter and I squirmed, longing for him to plunge his wonderfully thick cock deep inside me. Mick slapped me again and I reveled in the sensations the pain sent to my clit. Then I remembered the paint stirrer and the fear returned.

Straddling my waist, he pulled my t-shirt over my head and unfastened my bra. When he had stripped me, Mick stood up, grabbed my legs, and flipped me over on my back. In minutes, he had the four dog collars buckled around my wrists and ankles. I wriggled, dubious about this loss of control, the helplessness, and wondering if I should invoke the safeword before I got hurt. Mick stood beside the bed for a moment, his eyes running admiringly up and down my form. I couldn't resist the lust I saw, exhilarated that he directed it at me. *I've come this far, I can't quit now.* Then he covered my eyes with one of the folded bandanas, tying it behind my head. He fitted the other bandana into my mouth and secured it.

"I want to hear you say your safeword."

I found I could talk around the gag. "Monkeyshines," my voice sounded muffled, the word slurred.

"Don't say it again unless you mean it." I felt Mick's breath hot against my neck and I heard cellophane ripping open. One of the clothespins clamped down on my nipple and I squeaked around the gag. A moment later my other nipple knew the same, intense pain. I tugged at my bindings, squirming on the bed, but I had very little room to move.

Mick continued to apply clothespins, radiating in rows out from my areola. They stung, but none hurt as much as the ones on my nipples. He must have used the entire package--I have rather large breasts and Mick loves to play with them. He claimed that before we got together he used to jack off while thinking about my tits. Now, I wondered if he had imagined dozens of clothespins hanging from them.

For a very long moment, I neither heard nor felt anything new, just the pain in my nipples that started to dim as they became numb. Then, I caught the sound of a zipper and the thud of shorts laden with wallet and keys hitting the floor.

I imagined Mick's gorgeous long, thick dick pointing in my direction and longed to take the wonderfully smooth head in my mouth.

"Let's see which you like better, plastic or wood." Mick drew the paint stirrer along my outer thigh and then smacked the side of my ass.

The pain radiated through me, and surprised me by settling in my clit. I squirmed and arched my back, raising my pussy into the air, begging for his touch there. Mick slapped the side of my other cheek with the plastic spreader. That hurt much more than the wooden stirrer and my clit didn't respond. I felt Mick's chest pressing against my clothespinned breasts. "You like the plastic?" He ran the spreader up the inside of my thigh and teased my slit with it.

I shook my head.

"What about the wood?" Mick drew circles around my breasts with the paint stirrer.

I nodded, sheepishly. I couldn't believe that I enjoyed this.

Mick unfastened my ankles, pulled my legs up toward the head of the bed, and clipped them to the chains attached to my wrists. My thighs pressed the clothespins into my flesh, the collars on my ankles chafed against my skin. Mick whacked my ass again and again with the wooden paint stirrer. I squirmed and wriggled, but couldn't escape either the blows or the juices dripping from my pussy. I wondered if the paint stirrer would leave red marks and if I would have problems later sitting at my desk for hours on end. I decided I didn't care.

Finally, the blows ceased and I waited, trembling, my ass tingling, every inch of my skin sensitive to Mick. I felt him kneel in front of me and his hot breath caressed my inner thighs. I so longed for his touch, I wiggled my ass. The paint stirrer smacked me right between my nether lips. I yelped and jumped. But then, I moaned from the need the pain exacerbated.

"You're mine. I decide if you get touched there, when,

and for how long." He pulled my lips apart and blew on my clit. I swear I almost came, I was so tense at that point. Mick laughed. It was not the gentle chuckle I enjoyed hearing when the dog caught a frisbee or my cats chased each other around the couch in the living room. It had a sinister edge to it and I trembled in fear and excitement.

His tongue slid through my slit and teased my clit. I couldn't help myself and pushed my hips upward. He slapped me hard with his open hand, cupping his fingers so the pain radiated nearly as far as the thrill.

I whimpered.

"You will stay still unless I tell you to move."

I needed his touch. I wanted him to lick me or fuck me or something. I kept perfectly still. Finally, his tongue touched my clit again and I moaned. He licked me until the tension built and I could have come in another second. Then he stopped. I screamed in frustration, but he just laughed, that same wicked laugh. He teased me with his tongue, always stopping just before I exploded, until I didn't think I could stand another second.

For a moment, I lost all sense of him and then I heard the glorious sound of a condom package ripping open. Mick's sheathed dick found its way inside my sopping wet pussy and I sobbed with relief. He slammed in and out, pounding against my clit, until I exploded in the most intense orgasm I have ever known. It lasted forever while he continued shagging me, hard. I thought I would faint from over-stimulation when Mick cried out and shuddered. In all the times we had made love during the past four months, he had never once shouted when he came.

I could feel Mick's cock throbbing inside me. He shuddered again and again. When he finally finished, he unfastened all my collars and removed the clothespins from my breasts. I gasped when he took the ones off my nipples, sensation flowing back into the numb flesh sending ripples of pain and pleasure through me. At last, he removed the blindfold and kissed my eyelids while he pulled off the gag. His mouth found mine and our tongues danced together in my mouth.

Mick stretched out next to me and pulled me against him so my head lay on his shoulder and he wrapped his arms around me.

"I had no idea." I hadn't expected to enjoy the experience, only went along with it to keep Mick happy.

He grinned. "I'm glad you liked it. That's why I've been distant recently. I didn't know how to bring up the idea, afraid you would think I was some kind of pervert and run away from me. But well..." he ran his fingers through my hair, "as much as I enjoy making love to you, Eleanor, after a while plain vanilla gets a little boring. I can get my kink fix surfing BDSM sites on the Internet, but I would rather spend that time with you."

"I like vanilla. I don't mind getting kinky once in a while, but not every day, okay?" I didn't know how often I could survive the intensity I had just experienced.

"Don't worry. I promise not to tie you up more than once a week." Mick kissed me and I wrapped my arms around his neck.

The Things We Do for Love

By I.G. Frederick

I hadn't seen Liz in almost six years, not since she left Oregon, and her husband. Then, I had a hard time accepting her willingness to walk away from her marriage. Now, I could only empathize, since I'd divorced my own spouse. She certainly looked more gorgeous than ever. Her once brown hair had lightened to a golden blond and her bright green eyes sparkled.

She settled on the couch and I uncorked a bottle of Erath pinot noir I'd saved for a special occasion. I wanted to remind her of what she'd missed with only California wines to drink.

Liz held the glass up to her nose and inhaled. "You really know how to make a girl glad to come home."

"Obviously, you've enjoyed the California sun." I tipped my glass toward her tanned legs.

She shrugged. "Believe it or not, I've missed the rain. I've

31

especially missed all the bright flowers and lush greenery. Drought gets awfully boring."

I nodded. "Part of why I like the coast. Sunnier than the valley, but still more color and green than California." I sipped at the taste of cherries and currants, savoring the spicy finish. "So, tell me, what've you been up to down there besides cavorting in the sunshine? Any new love interests?"

Liz's eyes darkened for a moment and she cringed. I decided to change the subject and avoid mentioning the hot young stud next door. "Where were you working?"

She laughed. "Believe it or not, I've spent the last five years as a civilian employee at Edwards Air Force base. How about you? Why in the world are you doing in this two-bit town?"

I grinned but didn't mention that I'd fallen in love with my next-door neighbor even before I put an offer on my small townhome. "I work freelance. These days, most people don't care where you're located, as long as you can get their work done quickly and inexpensively."

"And, I suppose you can live cheaper here than in Portland?"

I shook my head. "Actually, no. The cost of living's pretty high. This place set me back as much as something the same size in the Pearl, but there's no fancy restaurants or upscale shops in walking distance. With fewer distractions, I get things done faster."

"I assume that view makes it all worthwhile?" Liz pointed at the distant waves visible from my front window.

I smiled. *That, and the one next door.* "Plus walking on the beach every day if I want." And, I ate healthier without tempting bakeries and food carts on every corner.

"Wish I could break free of city life and hang out in a tiny town." She smiled. "But, I'm not as talented as you. Not much call for administrative assistants online."

"You'd be surprised." I finished my wine and refilled both our glasses. "But, working for yourself means spending half your time selling your services. And, it helps to have resources for slow periods and times when the check's in the mail."

Liz gave me a weak smile. "Unfortunately, I've barely got enough green left to get a place to live. I need a job."

At that moment, Mick bounded in with Nora and planted a big kiss on my lips. Nora put her paws on my lap, her 'come take a walk with us' look on her face. "We're gonna head towards Cape Perpetua. You lovely ladies care to join us?" He held out his hand toward Liz. "Hi, I'm Mick."

Liz stuck both her hands under her thighs and glared at him.

May as well let Liz know what's going on. "Thanks, lover," I said aloud. "But, we've just started catching up. You're still making us dinner tonight, aren't you?" When he found out my friend was coming to visit, Mick had trucked up to Newport for bags full of special ingredients.

Liz cleared her throat. "I'd hoped to treat Eleanor this evening."

Mick's face drooped and he chewed on his lower lip. Then he grinned and a wicked glint lit up his green eyes. "Why don't you two enjoy girls' night out. I'll cook for you tomorrow. Everything I bought will keep until then." He leaned over and nibbled my earlobe. "See you later, pet."

Liz and I had a lovely dinner at the resort, although I insisted we go Dutch. She didn't ask me about Mick until I explained that rather than having her sleep on the couch, she'd get my bed while I went next door to Mick's.

"Isn't he kinda young for you?"

"He's not as young as he looks." I turned down the bed.

Liz pulled a hairbrush from her suitcase. "Still, when did you become a cougar?"

"Technically, not until three month ago when I turned forty. But, Mick and I started seeing each other before then."

She pulled the brush across her long hair and glared at me.

"Well, sleep tight." I pointed to the phone on the nightstand. "If you need me, Mick's number's on speed dial."

She scowled and kept brushing her hair.

I found Mick sitting at his desk, playing Morrowind. Kissing the back of his neck, I inhaled the faint scent of Irish Spring still lingering from his morning shower.

He saved all the loot he'd collected and shut down the game. "She has the hots for you."

I just stared at him. He turned his chair toward me. "She dissed me, didn't she?"

"Well, she thinks you're too young for me," I shrugged my shoulders "but so do I."

He narrowed his eyes.

"No, I won't go there. I just can't say that she dissed you," I held my fingers up to wrap quotes around the word "based on that. And, it's not like we talked about you all evening. You didn't come up until I told her I was sleeping here."

"She probably wishes you stayed there with her."

"That's ridiculous." I started for the bedroom.

Mick grabbed my wrist, pulling me back in his lap. "Don't tell me you wouldn't want to run your hands through her long, lovely locks." He pulled his fingers through my grey-streaked, red hair. "And kiss the wonderfully soft skin of her neck." His lips burned a path from my earlobe to my collarbone, but ice teased the edges of my mind.

"I'm sure you'd love to suck on those firm tits." He unbuttoned my shirt and licked around the lace of my bra while he reached around to unhook it.

The ice settled in my heart. He was the one with the hots -- for Liz. Not that I could blame him. Liz and Mick would have made the perfect blond-beauty couple. And she was only three years older than him, not nine. I pulled away and stood up. "I'm straight."

Mick shook his head. "You've got to be kidding? I've seen you look at other women."

Because, I'm comparing myself to them and wondering why you chose me. Aloud, I said: "Usually, I see something I wish I had."

Mick rose and wrapped his muscular arms around me. "Why'd you want to look like anyone else? You're beautiful." He pressed his lips to mine and I melted. I could never resist gorgeous Mick. He overloaded my senses until I could no longer think of anything but my need for him.

He removed his shirt and mine and I relished the touch of his hot skin pressed against my breasts. I stroked his back and he slid his hands into my shorts. "Sure you're not the least bit curious about making love to another woman?"

I refrained from shaking my head vigorously. "Never really thought about it," I muttered.

Mick scooped me up and carried me to the bedroom, stripped off the rest of my clothing and his. He lowered his head to my breasts and teased my nipples to hardness. His hands caressed my skin, finding all the spots he knew would send me spinning. I was sopping wet by the time he nudged me face down on the bed, pulled my hips up, and plunged inside me. We both moaned. I gasped when he reached around to hold my heavy breasts, tweaking my nipples with his thumbs.

I pressed my lips together to keep from crying out loud -- whatever Liz had against Mick, no need to rub her face in our relationship. He thrust faster and harder, building up pressure on my G-spot, making my clit long for contact. Finally, he slid one hand down to finger it and I came hard, clenching around his cock until he exploded inside me. I slid down onto my stomach. Mick, resting his weight on his forearms, kissed my neck until I stopped shaking.

I woke to discover Mick had covered me with a blanket and snuggled up beside me, one arm across my back. He grinned when he saw my eyes open. "If she does have the hots for you, would you consider a three-way?"

I cringed. *At least, now the truth will come out.*

"Nah." He shrugged. "I'll bet she's a lesbo. Really, I just want to watch. Whaddya think?"

I couldn't even pick up my head to look at him. I had no

clue how to respond. I'd never had any desire to get sexually involved with a female, with or without an audience. On the other hand, the idea didn't gross me out. I'd already done previously unimaginable things to keep Mick happy. I sighed. Maybe Liz would turn us down.

In the morning, Mick made pancakes and I went to fetch Liz. She wore a form-hugging white tee and green shorts that showed off long, slim legs. Her gym-toned body made her look years younger than her age. I decided to be grateful Mick just wanted to watch.

I crossed my arms under my breasts. *May as well get it over with.* "Mick came up with the most outrageous notion."

She grimaced, but I blurted it out before she could stop me. "He thinks you don't like him 'cause you've got the hots for me." I jammed my hands into the pocket of my denim shorts. "Silly, I know. Come on, let's go eat."

I opened the door, but Liz still sat on the couch. "Mick's not as dumb as he looks."

I leaned against the wall to keep from falling over.

"Ever wonder why I never introduced you to the lover I left my husband for?"

I managed to turn my head from one side to the other, but it took effort.

She uncrossed her long legs and rose gracefully to her feet. "I've always had the hots for you, Eleanor."

"Mick wants to watch." My voice came out in a squeak.

Liz laughed and stepped close enough for our tits to touch. "And what do you think about that?" She ran her fingers through my hair.

I shrugged. "I've enjoyed other things he's convinced me to try." Fortunately, my voice sounded almost normal.

Mick stepped out of his front door with a pancake turner in one hand and a hot pad in the other. "Hey gals, breakfast's ready."

Liz tugged my hair until our lips touched and she plunged her tongue into my mouth. Her other hand slipped around to my ass. She pulled us together and I could feel her erect nipples.

Mick cleared his throat. "I can stick the pancakes in the oven if you two want to eat first."

Liz stepped back. "No, let's have breakfast. We should discuss ground rules."

My knees were so weak I had to lean against the wall again. Mick put his arm around my waist and helped me over to his place.

The smell of coffee revived me a bit. He handed me a steaming mug and guided me to one of the bar stools at his kitchen counter. Liz planted a kiss on the back of my neck, which did not help my equilibrium, before climbing onto the stool next to mine.

Mick set stacks of pancakes smothered in blueberry compote in front of us. They smelled heavenly and tasted even better.

Liz swallowed a forkfull. "Yum. Glad you finally found a man who could cook."

We both laughed. My ex couldn't boil water to save his life.

I sipped at the coffee between bites of rich lusciousness.

Liz looked up at Mick. "I'm not bi. I tried to survive straight and almost lost my mind. Six years ago, I finally admitted I preferred women when I fell in love with a Lieutenant and followed her to California." She poured milk into her coffee cup. "Unfortunately, she was already married to the Air Force. I finally gave up and I'm moving back home."

Mick handed her the sugar bowl. "Look, I'm pretty good at reading folks and I figured you weren't into guys. No offense, but you're not my type anyway." He ran one finger down my cheek and I had to smile.

Liz spooned sugar into her cup. "None taken, since you're not mine."

Mick tucked into his own plate of fruity goodness. "I'd just love to see Eleanor getting it on with another woman.

Maybe you'd let her suck me at some point, but I promise I won't touch you."

Liz twirled a bit of pancake in the blueberries. "You can watch from the chair as long as you keep your clothes on. If you don't get in my way ..." she shrugged her shoulders.

"Deal." Mick extended his hand and this time Liz took it. I felt like a piece of meat handed over, but my panties were wet.

Mick stacked empty plates in the sink. "Here or there?"

Liz slid off the stool. "I have toys in my suitcase."

Mick opened the front door, bowed us through, and followed us across the porch. I fumbled with my keys and dropped them twice before Mick retrieved them and ushered us inside. He followed us back to the bedroom and settled into the rocking chair.

Liz pulled me into her arms and kissed me. I let my hands slide around her waist. I decided I liked the feel of her curves pressed into mine, although Liz's were definitely less pronounced than my own. She caressed my rear and ground her crotch against my leg. For the first time, I smelled the scent of arousal other than my own.

I let my fingers wander over her firm ass and wondered how much time she spent in the gym. Liz pulled my tee shirt over my head and unhooked my bra. Apparently she shared Mick's fascination with my ample bosom because she licked my breasts all over and teased my nipples with her tongue. My eyes rolled back in my head as the delicious sensation spread warmth to my clit.

She guided me toward the bed and I fell backwards onto the comforter. My shorts and panties disappeared and, for a moment, so did Liz. I heard her rummaging around in her suitcase then she lay next to me on the bed, naked. I reached out to touch her breast and her nipple hardened against my palm. The soft, smooth skin felt good in my hand, although her pert tit barely filled it. I leaned in and stuck out my tongue. Her skin tasted slightly salty and I picked up the scent of jasmine lotion.

I took a deep breath and wrapped my lips around her nipple. I'm not sure which of us got hotter from my suckling. I'd never imagined a woman could feel this good. Liz put her leg between mine and I rubbed my clit against her thigh. She pushed it into me harder and my juices trickled down her leg. With both hands, she wove her fingers into my hair and rolled me onto my back. My head hung over the side of the bed as she kissed her way from my neck, to my breasts and down to my belly. I opened my legs and lifted my hips a little, eager for the touch of her tongue.

Mick stood behind my head, unzipped his fly and pulled out his magnificent cock. My mouth watered just looking at it. The head touched my lips at the same time Liz's tongue found my clit and I screamed in delight. I sucked his cock into my mouth while Liz sent wave after wave of pleasure coursing through me. She licked, she sucked, she even nibbled my clit with her teeth. I just shook and tried hard not to bite down.

Then I felt something rigid pressing against my nether lips. Liz lay across me, her breasts pressing against mine, fucking me with some sort of dildo. I exploded and so did Mick, filling my mouth with hot juicy come. I swallowed every drop and licked him and my lips clean. He stepped back and Liz nibbled my ear. Then she swung her legs around and straddled my face, leaning over so she could slide the dildo in and out of my dripping cunt.

She smelled like honey and I stuck my tongue out to lick up some of the hot nectar dripping on my face. I had to admit I liked the taste of Mick's come better, but she sure was a luscious second best. I plunged in, exploring the shape of her cunt with my mouth. She had thinner lips and a bigger clit than I, but I had no trouble figuring out how to please her. She came twice, gushing all over my face. Meanwhile, that dildo plunging in and out of my pussy set me off again.

When she finally stretched out next to me, we were both covered with a sheen of sweat and sticky with each others' come. We wrapped our arms around each other and I enjoyed the heat of her skin against mine while our breathing slowly returned to normal. Once again, Mick had talked me into doing something I would never have tried otherwise. I had to wonder what else he might come up with in the future.

Paid in Full

By I.G. Frederick & Patrick

After almost a year together, Mick and I don't bother knocking on each other's doors anymore, so I waltzed into his townhome one summer afternoon to see if he wanted to go for a walk on the beach. I was a little taken aback when I found two gorgeous hunks sitting on his brown leather sofa instead of one. They presented a study in contrasts. Mick with his long blond hair falling loose over his shoulders, earrings in his left ear, and Native American tattoos on his arms wore cutoffs, a black tee shirt, and flip flops. The stranger, whose short dark hair was cropped tight against his head, had no visible body art and wore cammie pants and shirt with spit-polished black combat boots.

Bowls of tortilla chips, bean dip, and salsa sat on the glass coffee table and they each held a half empty bottle of Rogue Ale Black Lager. Mick dangled his by the neck from two fingers, the other man kept a firm grip on the bottle itself.

"Eleanor, my sweet." Mick reached out both hands and when I took them he pulled me across his lap, facing his

43

friend. "This is my buddy, Jack. We served in the Third Battalion together, although he wasn't smart enough to bail after one tour and ended up in Afghanistan and Iraq."

Jack reached over, took one of my hands, and kissed my fingers. "Pleased to meet you, pretty lady." His blue eyes cut through me like ice. "Why would you hang out with a coward and a deserter when you could have yourself a real man who's proudly served his country for more than a decade?"

"Because she needs a man who can satisfy her, not one who runs off to play soldier every time Halliburton wants more profits." Mick wrapped his strong arms around me and I leaned into his chest.

"You don't deserve such a beautiful woman." Jack winked at me and I must admit I batted my eyelashes at him, flirting shamelessly. I look pretty good these days. Between long walks on the beach with Mick and working out in the gym he built in his garage, I've toned my legs and flattened my tummy. I even dye my hair now to hide the ever widening grey streaks. The appreciative looks I get from fellows about town, and having a lover nine years my junior, have done wonders for my self confidence.

Mick hugged me tighter. "Fortunately, she doesn't agree with you." He kissed the curve of my neck where it meets my shoulders, sending an electrifying jolt through me.

"How do you know? She's probably just staying with you until I came along." Jack moved closer and ran the tip of one finger up my bare leg. I shivered. "See?" He took my hand again and this time planted his burning lips on the inside of my wrist. I'm sure he felt my pulse speed up. "Tell you what. Since I can only stay 'til tomorrow, I'll make you a deal. You know that five hundred you owe me? Let me spend the night with this beautiful creature and I'll call it even."

I gasped. I don't know what was more disconcerting, the fact that he was trying to seduce me while Mick held me in his arms or that Jack thought sex with me was worth hundreds of dollars. I knew Mick could ill afford to pay up. His company had laid him off and hired him back as a part-time subcontractor three months ago, so he was hurting for cash. He'd even talked about renting out his place and moving in next door with me, although with both of us working at home from our spare bedroom offices that seemed a bit impractical.

Still, I didn't believe for a minute that Mick would take him up on the offer. He claimed to love me. Although he'd enjoyed watching me have sex with a woman, I was sure another man would be a different story.

To my surprise, Mick laughed long and hard. His fingers found the buttons of my shirt and slowly undid first one, then another. "Only if I get to watch."

My eyes widened, my mouth fell partially open, and I sat there in shock. But, I could feel Mick getting hard under my ass and my own moisture seeping into my panties.

"Watch? Hell," Jack slowly eased his lips along the inside of my arm from my wrist to my elbow, sending a shiver down my spine, "why don't you join in? She ever had a DP?"

Mick undid the next button, exposing my cleavage and the lacy top of my black bra. "I doubt it. She wasn't terribly daring until I captured her." He ran a finger lightly between my exposed breasts and memories of the sexual adventures he'd persuaded me to participate in intensified the heat between my legs.

Kissing my neck, Mick undid another button. Jack leaned over and licked my breasts above the lace, then buried his nose between them. "Sweet." His breath tickled my skin.

Mick unhooked my bra, Jack pushed it up out of his way and sucked one nipple into his mouth while Mick pinched the other. I moaned.

A year ago, I would have taken offense at two men discussing how they would use me sexually while ignoring the fact that I was sitting right there. But, Mick's attitude that he owned me and could share me with his friend, Jack's willingness to give up five hundred dollars to get his cock inside me, and the thought of having sex with two gorgeous men at once all turned me on too much to care.

Mick undid the last button of my shirt and slid his hand down into my shorts. He wiggled one finger in between my nether lips, pulling it the length of my slit, and drew it back out glistening with my wetness.

Jack inhaled my scent and smiled. "I think we can accept this as evidence of the lady's consent."

Chuckling, Mick unzipped my shorts and slid them and my panties down to my knees. Jack removed my sandals and pulled my clothes off my legs, tossing them aside. "Shall we adjourn to the bedroom?"

"Of course." Mick stood, lifting me to my feet. He pulled off my shirt and bra and dropped them on the sofa. Scooping me up with one arm under my knees and the other behind my back, he carried me into the bedroom. Jack followed, unbuttoning his shirt as he walked.

Mick laid me across the red and black afghan covering his bed, its texture was rough against my bare skin. Jack tossed his shirt on the floor, revealing a hard muscular chest, criscrossed with half a dozen white scars. He knelt to unlace his boots while Mick stripped off his own clothing.

Mick pulled open the drawer of his nightstand, grabbed a strip of condoms and tossed them to Jack. He extracted the half-full lube bottle and waved it. "Back or front?"

I stared up at two impressive hard-ons aiming at each other from either side of the bed. Mick's was thicker, but Jack's was longer. I licked my lips in expectation and they both laughed.

Mick tossed the lube down beside my hand and Jack knelt near my head. I turned to caress the head of his penis with my tongue, enjoying the salty male taste of his skin. I closed my eyes, made my mouth into an O, and allowed Jack to ease himself between my lips. I lost track of Mick until he thrust his rod between my nether lips and I groaned in delight around Jack's cock. The two of them countered each other's rhythm, one pushing in as the other pulled back. I lay there, writhing in pleasure as their cocks slid in and out of me, massaging my most sensitive spots.

Mick leaned over and sucked one of my nipples into his mouth, sending me over the edge. My body trembled and my pussy clenched around his cock. I sucked Jack even deeper into my mouth, lips working up and down his shaft. They both shouted and pumped their seed into me: Jack's sticky sweet come slithering down my throat, Mick's load gushing into my cunt then trickling out to drip down my ass.

Stretching out behind me, pressing his chest against my back, Mick played with my breasts, flicking my still hard nipples with his thumb. He licked my neck. I wiggled in anticipation and both men laughed again.

Jack lay on his side, one hand caressing my hip, and kissed me. I tasted malt mixed with salsa. "She always this insatiable?"

Mick pushed his groin against my ass and I could feel him getting hard again. "Why do you think I keep her around?" I might have found his words insulting, if he didn't profess his love for me daily. I figured he was just bragging for his buddy and given how much I was enjoying the encounter, I saw no reason to contradict him.

Jack pushed aside Mick's hand from one of my breasts. His tongue licked my areola and slid down my flesh to my chest. His lips returned to my nipple and sucked it into his mouth and teased the hard nub with his teeth. I squirmed, pushing my hips toward his, my cunt pulsing with need. Jack ripped open a condom package and slipped it over his long, erect rod. Behind me, I heard the splurt of lube hitting Mick's palm which made my ass wiggle in anticipation. Mick eased his lubricated cock into my ass from behind then reached around and held my pussy lips open in invitation. Jack gripped my hips and slid into the wet heat of my cunt with a contented sigh.

I floated in an ecstasy of intense sensations: hot, hard

chests pressed against my back and breasts; long, thick cocks, stroking the deliciously swollen tissue inside my cunt and ass; hands (I no longer knew whose) squeezing my breasts; hot lips on my neck and mouth. I couldn't have moved if I'd needed to, but fortunately this position didn't require any effort on my part. Their skin burned mine, the scent of their sweat mingled with my own hot juices, and the pounding of three hearts in my ears drowned out even their heavy breathing and grunts.

I was dizzy with sensory overload that settled in my clit until I exploded, my entire body twitching while the two of them drove in and out of me. I lay shuddering when first Jack and then Mick grunted and I felt them spasm inside me, their come captured by their condoms. The three of us lay tangled together, panting until Jack slipped out and Mick eased free of my ass.

Flopping onto his back, Jack put his shoulder under my head. "Damn, Mick was right. You are one hot number." He made a sizzling sound between his teeth. "I'm not supposed to tell you this, but Mick made up the whole thing about him owing me five hundred dollars to spice things up a bit. Now, though, I'm wondering if you knew what he did, you might leave this bad boy for me."

I could only giggle and shake my head. How could I be upset with Mick when I'd enjoyed every moment so much?

Jack kissed my forehead. 'Tell you what, little lady: if Mick here ever gets tired of you, look me up, okay?"

"No fucking way, dude." Mick ran one hand from my thigh, across my hip to my waist. "This one's a keeper. I might share her occasionally, but I'll never let her go."

I leaned back against him, his words as comforting to my soul as his hand was soothing my heated skin.

Renovations
By I.G. Frederick & Patrick

For more than a month, the whirr of a power saw, pounding of hammer against nails, and thunk of an electric stapler have emanated from my garage. Mick emerges at the end of the day, sweaty and covered with sawdust and paint. But, he won't let me see what he's been doing.

He's turned his townhome over to a vacation rental agency. We swapped out much of his stuff for mine -- his is a lot nicer, since I let my ex have most of the good stuff when I left Portland. We both kept all our office furniture, of course, and we found a couple of inexpensive twin beds for his second bedroom.

Nora has finally stopped barking when vacationers moved in to "her place" for a weekend or a week. The cats no longer screech every time she bounds into a room, instead they've decided her tail makes a good toy. But, Mick still disappears into the garage for hours at a time. He drives up to Newport and comes home with the bed of his pickup truck filled with lumber, wallboard, paint cans, carpet rolls, and bags full of things that rattle and clang. UPS and FedEx deliver package after package of various shapes and sizes. They all disappear behind the locked door in the kitchen.

Until two days ago, his desk and computer were crowding the small living room and I was eager to see them move into whatever he's building in the garage. With two adults, two cats, and a Border Collie, the house was crowded enough without extra furniture.

Finally, at the end of a rainy windy day that presumably had kept the vacationers next door glued to their window watching the storm, Mick emerged. He smelled of paint and varnish and had a glint in his eye. After he locked the door, he turned to me. "It's finally finished. I'm going to get cleaned up. You open a bottle of wine and we'll celebrate the grand opening."

While Mick showered, I uncorked my last bottle of Erath pinot noir and arranged some cheese, crackers, dried figs, and carrots on a platter. I knew Mick had forgotten to eat lunch and figured I'd better make sure he had something to munch on with the wine.

I felt him behind me as I added a few olives. "Nice touch, babe." He wrapped his arms around my waist and planted his lips against the curve of my neck, burning my skin until I melted back against him. Even after almost two years, Mick's touch always sent a jolt of desire through me.

He released me and I had to grab the counter for a moment. "But, that can wait. I want to show you what I've done." He snatched a piece of cheese then grabbed the platter in one hand, extracting his keys from the pocket of his khaki shorts with the other. I followed him with wine bottle and glasses.

The door opened on a room that couldn't have taken up more than a third of what had been my garage. Two other doors, both closed, led out of it: one in the wall separating his garage from mine, and one in a new wall that stretched across the width of the garage. A floor-to-ceiling bookcase extended from the house to the new wall at one end of the room. His desk faced the house and filing cabinets and a storage cabinet filled the space between the book cases and the door along the new wall. On the other side of the door, hooks and brackets held our combined collection of tools for yard work and house maintenance. Opposite them, on the wall against the house, he'd built a workbench. He had covered the cement floor in a utilitarian grey-blue office carpet.

Mick set the platter down on his desk and opened the door between the two garages. "Now, we can access the gym without having to go outside in the rain." He had changed the lock on the door to his townhome so it couldn't be accessed from that house, and we had been using the overhead garage door to gain entry.

Closing the door, Mick poured wine into the glasses. He took one and clinked it against mine. I sipped at the taste of cherries and currants while staring at him, waiting for whatever was behind that third door. He piled some cheese slices on a water cracker, topped it with an olive, and popped it into his mouth. The gleam brightened his green eyes and his damp hair had wet the shoulders of the tee shirt that molded itself to his muscular chest and arms.

Since it was obvious he was going to make me wait, I helped myself to a slice of Muenster and a fig, the salty sweet combination enhanced by the wine's spicy finish. After he'd emptied a good third of the tray and his glass, Mick took mine and set them both down on the desk.

"Now, for the pièce de resistance." Mick flung open the door in the middle of the new wall, reached in, and flipped a light switch. I stepped through the door and gasped. Rich, oak paneling covered the walls and plush, burgundy carpet the floor. Track lighting pointed at the ceiling, brightening the room without creating glare. Electric baseboard heaters had warmed the varnish-scented air.

An X-shaped cross stood in the far corner, a massage table and an odd shaped bench were set against the outer wall. Large hooks protruded from the ceiling and the wall covering what used to be the overhead garage door. The wall between the two garages had an array of implements that made my knees weak: whips in various shapes and configurations, leather cuffs, blindfolds, ball gags, chains, skeins of rope in every color imaginable, paddles in various sizes and shapes. There were other items I couldn't identify, and I wasn't sure I wanted to. A cedar chest and big pillows lined the wall underneath them.

I had fallen against Mick's chest and he held me up with his hands cupped around my ample breasts. I sucked in air, realizing I'd stopped breathing while I took in everything he had done to my garage.

He kissed my neck. "In this room, I am your Master." His voice, deep and husky, sent a chill through my spine. "You will kneel in my presence unless given permission to stand. You will speak only if given permission." He lowered his voice even more. "You will come only when I tell you that you may." He let go of me, and I sank to my knees on the padded carpet, mostly because they couldn't support me without his assistance. "And, unless I've provided you with a costume to wear, you will never again set foot in this room with clothing on. Understood?"

"Yes, Master," I whispered. I pulled my tee shirt over my head and reached behind my back to unhook my bra. Mick held out his hand and I handed him my garments.

"You may stand to finish undressing." His voice brooked no disobedience. Besides, I didn't want to disobey. I liked that he had created a separate space where we could slip into the dynamic that had built ever since that fateful trip to the Mercantile so many months ago. Sometimes, I wanted him to take command and sometimes I wanted the pain he could give me.

I pushed myself to my feet and slipped out of my loafers, jeans, and already damp panties, handing each garment to Mick. I pulled off my stocks and dropped back to my knees. When he's not playing Master, Mick is the sweetest, most considerate lover/partner a woman could want. But, he has a cruel sadistic side, that, I'm forced to admit, turns me on.

Mick extracted my panties from the pile in his arms, held them to his face, and inhaled. He smiled. "Glad you appreciate my efforts."

"Yes, Master. Thank you, Master for this beautiful dungeon."

He disappeared through the doorway for a moment and returned without my clothing, holding the platter. He sat in front of me cross legged, the platter on the floor between us. "You didn't eat lunch either, did you?"

I shook my head. I'd had a five p.m. deadline for a big project, so I'd only gotten up from my computer for bathroom breaks and to catch a momentary glimpse of the storm through the living room window. He wrapped a slice of cheese around a carrot and topped it with an olive. I opened my mouth and enjoyed the crunch of the sweet carrot, with the salty sharp taste of cheese and the tang of the olive.

Mick ate one of his creations. "Help yourself, babe. We don't want to play on empty stomachs."

When the platter was empty, he pushed it toward the door, and stood behind me. In one smooth move, he ran his fingers though my hair, grabbed a handful near my head, and pulled me to my feet and into his arms. He ran his free hand down my neck and cupped my breast, pinching my nipple between his fingers. I squirmed, the pain traveling, as it always did, straight to my clit.

"For the inauguration of our new dungeon, I'm going to let you pick: cross, table, or spanking bench?"

I wanted to ask which one would get me fucked the most, but dared not. I wasn't ready to take a beating standing up, and the massage table didn't look like it would take both our weights. "Bench." I thought I'd said it out loud, but it came out as a hoarse whisper.

Still holding my hair, Mick kissed my neck. "You got it, babe." He dragged me over to the bench and forced me into a kneeling position on the extensions with my chest resting on the center section. My body fit the bench perfectly. The leather padding made it relatively comfortable and felt cool against my skin. He must have custom made the bench for me.

Mick attached cuffs to my wrists and ankles and clipped them to eye bolts on the bench, pinning them into place. My head hung over the end, my arms were secured to either side, and my rear was sticking up in the air. He covered my eyes with a soft velvety blindfold and tied it around my head.

I felt him caress my ass and I pushed against his hands, eager for his touch. Then pain shot through me as lacquered wood connected with both my cheeks. I gasped. He rubbed the paddle against my skin, letting the sensation flow through me, then drew back and hit me again. My clit pulsed in response. I wanted more, needed more. He gave it to me. I lost count of the number of times the paddle connected, but I could feel the heat grow across my ass. The paddle was smoother and sturdier than the wooden paint stirrer he had used the first time we had played. Its lacquered finish felt good and delivered a wider, more even and aching pain.

He grabbed my hair, lifting my head, and pressed his cock against my lips until I opened my mouth. He stuffed it in and I moaned in delight. My ass and my cunt ached with need, but one of them would get filled eventually. Meanwhile, I loved the taste of him, the feel of his smooth skin against my tongue, the hard shaft penetrating my lips, the tickle of Irish Spring scented pubic hair when he pressed against my face. I relaxed and let him slide deep into my throat.

Strips of leather dragged slowly across my shoulders. They lifted and I felt the thud of a flogger against my skin and a deep aching pain spread across back. Tingles of desire coursed through me. I moaned and Mick chuckled. He alternated thrusting his cock down my throat and whipping my back. The leather struck between my legs. I clenched my fingers to keep from coming. I couldn't ask for permission with a mouth full of cock, but that combined with the pain had pushed me to the brink. He hit my pussy again with flogger and I groaned in need. That pushed Mick over the edge and hot, sticky jizz burst into my throat. I gulped it down eagerly.

He stroked my hair. "Good girl." Mick pulled out and I extended my tongue to lick a bit of his sweet salty goodness off my lips. He knelt down to kiss me and sent another jolt of desire coursing through me.

"Please, Master," I managed to whisper.

"Soon, precious. Soon." He pushed a ball gag into my mouth, fastened the strap around my head. He stepped away. I could hear rustling over by the wall with all the implements of pain and pleasure.

Short sharp parallel lines of pain erupted across the inside of my thighs. I recognized the small flogger he had purchased to celebrate the one-year anniversary of the first time we made love. Although, only six inches long, the half-inch wide strips raised fresh agony from my sensitive skin. The leather moved closer and closer to my dripping wet cunt. I opened my legs as wide as I could, straining against the ankle cuffs. Finally, Mick dragged the tails through my open lips and I wriggled in anticipation. I cried out as three quick strokes, against that most sensitive area, erupted in brilliant pain. Through the haze of pain and pleasure I heard him say: "You may come now." Released, I exploded, my whole body shaking, my scream muffled by the rubber ball in my mouth.

I heard the flogger hit the floor. Mick's hands gripped each side of my ass and the hard length of his cock slid deep into my slick cunt. The edge of his fingernails raked across the welts on my backside. I hoped permission to come wasn't limited to one time, because the pain and his cock banging against my g-spot sent me into spasms of ecstasy again and again. I'd lost track of how many times when he shot his load inside me.

What seemed like hours later, I was vaguely aware of Mick removing the cuffs and lifting me off the bench. I floated in bliss while he cuddled me and we lounged against the pillows, velvety soft against my ravaged skin. I realized that a fleece blanket, smelling of cedar, had been draped around me.

Mick kissed my forehead. "I take it you like our new play space?"

It took all my energy to nod, but I was very grateful for what he'd done. The dungeon would give us a space to explore my masochism, while preventing my submission from spilling out into the rest of our lives.

Acknowledgements

This book would not have reached your hands without the help of many dear friends and colleagues. I thank my readers and supporters, especially Cindy, my proofreader, editor, and best friend. Thanks also to all those who have served me, well and ill, over the years. I have learned something from each one of you and I hope that you find what you seek.

Other fiction
by I.G. Frederick includes:

Complicated Couplings
Four sexy stories about tangled twosomes

"If You Love Someone" — *Tara leaves her husband to move in with Nathan, but he abandons her after a few months. When he returns, begging her to take him back, life and love look very different.*

"Commiserate" — *The same man dumped them both. When they commiserate, they discover more in common than an ex-boyfriend.*

"Passion's Price" — *Richard steals Gina's heart from three thousand miles away. But, when he moves across the country, her intensity and passion for life drive him away.*

"Lunchtime Lover" — *Both married, they started their affair with the promise never to fall in love. Then Lisa's divorce becomes final.*

www.eroticawriter.net/ComplicatedCouplings.html

Cougar Conquests
Beautiful older women on the prowl and the sweet young cubs captured by their allure

"Benjamin" — *A chance meeting at a munch in a tiny town leads Benjamin to an opportunity for training. But, Lady Gina tries to end the relationship rather than emotionally torture herself.*

"Festival of Eros" — *The handsome young man followed her around all evening, behaving like the perfect submissive ... until she learned his identity.*

"Paddles" — *A biker bar with no bikers? The decor, name, and patrons of a bar in a small Eastern Oregon town puzzle William who just stopped in for a beer. Then the owner introduces him to the secrets of this very special tavern.*

"Starting Over" - *When her pet walked out on her, she stayed away from parties because it hurt to watch other women playing with their toys. But, a friend coerces her into attending a unique event.*

"The Cougar and the College Boys" — *Alone in the woods, hours from Portland, Tess discovers four college friends staying in a nearby cabin. The boys invite her to share their campfire, their dinner, and ...*

www.eroticawriter.net/CougarConquests.html

Dommemoir

WARNING:
This book changes women's attitudes about relationship dynamics, forever.

In Geneviéve's journey of discovery she dabbles in the BDSM lifestyle which forces her to recognize and acknowledge her true nature. Her memoir, woven together with that of a male slave, draws the reader into an intense odyssey of sexual expression triumphing over sexual repression while delivering fascinating insight about a different kind of love.

"The aptly titled Dommemoir delivers on so many levels... It quickly sucks you in and envelopes you in the bondage of its spell... Dommemoir is a character study that breathes complex and compelling life into its hero, the devastating Lady Geneviéve and the fortunate submissives who worship at her feet... placing you in the delicious bondage of its dark and compelling landscape..."

*Larry Brooks, **USA Today** bestselling author of Darkness Bound **and** Bait and Switch*

www.eroticawriter.net/Dommemoir.html

Family Dynamics

Six sultry stories exploring sexuality in Dominant/submissive liaisons

"'Aunt' Grace" — Jen needed a place to stay in Portland and turned to her father's stepsister. But, she found so much more than she ever dreamed possible with her "Aunt" Grace. Second Place, NLA:I John Preston Short Story Award.

"Leather Family" — Kyle needs his own boy. Jacques would do almost anything to find a place in a Leather Family. But, Kyle serves a female Master.

"Searching" — Two dominants love each other, but need someone who submits to them both. Just how far will young Jeremy go to serve the lovely Lady Theresa?

"Taking Control" — To free the woman she loves from a horrid sadist's perverted games, Melanie must set aside her own aversion to men.

"Family Ties" — When her slave's ex faces eviction, Katherine offers refuge. But can Naomi pay the price?

"Said the Unicorn" — Tessa dedicates herself to her Master's service, so his determination to add another woman to their family devastates her.

www.eroticawriter.net/FamilyDynamics.html

Fork In The Road:

Changing people's lives, and relationships in three pairs of sexy stories

"Said the Unicorn" — Tessa dedicates herself to her Master's service, so his determination to add another woman to their family devastates her.

"Proposals" — The evening appears perfectly arranged for him to pop the question. But, Christopher's proposition takes Geraldine on an unanticipated sexual adventure.

"Winners & Losers" — When he finally walks away from the blackjack table, Jeffrey finds someone worth gambling on.

www.eroticawriter.net/ForkinRoad.html

Lessons Learned
Sometimes you need more than love

Four sizzling hot FemDom love stories about women who come to terms with their dominant sides and discover that makes them more attractive to the men they love.

"Tea Party" — What if the first time your best friend drags you to a FemDom "Tea Party" you see your former boyfriend serving canapes naked?

"Blind Date" — How do you respond when you find your ex-husband hanging out at the restaurant where you planned to meet your "Blind Date"?

"To Serve" — If you love a vanilla woman and you only want "To Serve," how do you introduce her to the lifestyle without scaring her away?

"Change in View" — What if a "Change in View" alters the attitude of the man you mentored so he could find his perfect Mistress?

www.eroticawriter.net/LessonsLearned.html

Love Hurts

but in a good way
five steamy stories about the dark side of love

"B&D Trainee" — *Online, Xavier promised to make his B&D fantasies come true. But, had he jumped in over his head?*

"Knife Play" — *Seeking a knife he saw online, Jack inadvertently found himself in a room full of pain and bondage contraptions. He almost turned around and left, but a beautiful woman taught him a different way to appreciate blades.*

"Pussy Whipped" — *Eric knew nothing about BDSM, but purchased a ticket to a fundraiser to help out his friends. When Miranda asks him to "play," he discovers exactly what those four letters mean.*

"The Auction" — *He attended the auction with only one goal — to acquire a very special whip. But an offer to try it out proved irresistible and he discovered sometimes events, and women, can exceed one's expectations.*

"FemDom Fairy Tale" — *A FemDom's offhand remark about a photograph at an erotic art show draws a handsome man's attention. But, when two dominants find each other attractive, which one chooses to kneel?*

www.eroticawriter.net/LoveHurts.html

Second Chances
Six sexy stories about getting a second shot at the gold ring

"Back to School" — *An admin error forces Jordan and Dennis to share a dorm room. Older than their classmates, they decide to stick together. But Jordan's past threatens to keep them apart.*

"Gordon" — *When the cover model of her latest book walks into the coffee shop where she writes, Lenore embarrassingly calls him by her character's name. His reaction confounds her.*

"Spa Date" — *Dismayed that she introduced Sam to the woman who betrayed her, Julie tries to fix her up again.*

"Salt for His Wounds" — *When Eleanor's ex-husband shows up begging for a second chance, she asks her young, gorgeous next door neighbor for a favor. Mick takes advantage of the opportunity.*

"Proposal — Tangled Webs" — *The evening appears perfectly arranged for him to pop the question. But, Christopher's proposition takes Geraldine on an unanticipated sexual adventure.*

"Starting Over" — *When her pet walked out on her, she stayed away from parties because it hurt to watch other women playing with their toys. But, a friend coerces her into attending a unique event.*

www.eroticawriter.net/SecondChances.html

When Two's Not Enough
Seven sexy ménage stories

"Tribal Fusion" — *Whenever and wherever he dances, Dominic collects propositions, but the Lady Lenore's proposal takes him by surprise.*

"Two Brothers" — *A divorcée in a flashy sports car attracts the attention of two young virgin brothers visiting the "big" city of Boise.*

"Honeymoon" — *Although she expected to honeymoon aboard a cruise ship, Allison finds herself sailing on a private yacht staffed by an incredibly beautiful couple. Believing her new husband wants to hide his older, less attractive wife, makes it difficult to enjoy the hedonistic delights offered in paradise.*

"Jail Bait" — *Serena wants Joshua to pop her cherry, but he won't touch her because of her age. When her birthday finally makes it legal, he arranges for a very special celebration.*

"Nikki's Birthday" — *Even someone happy in a monogamous relationship might find the gift of a hot, new toy for an evening of decadence incredibly exciting. (Inspired by a real birthday present given to a lovely little bi-sexual, genderqueer slave.)*

"Market Boy" — *When a beautiful Domme offers Jack the opportunity to serve at a party for her friends, he responds too quickly and too eagerly, getting more than he bargained for.*

"The Cougar and the College Boys" — *Alone in the*

woods, hours from Portland, Tess discovers four college friends staying in a nearby cabin. The boys invite her to share their campfire, their dinner, and ...

www.eroticawriter.net/TwoNotEnough.html

Young & Eager
Barely legal but hardly innocent

"Two Brothers" — *A divorcée in a flashy sports car attracts the attention of two young virgin brothers visiting the "big" city of Boise.*

"Teachers Pet" — *Trapped at an all-girls' school in the middle of nowhere, Sabrina tries to get her hunky teacher to bust her cherry.*

"Arresting Development" — *Bethany went out with Officer Rick to avoid a speeding ticket, but discovered she enjoyed getting "arrested."*

"Jail Bait" — *Serena wants Joshua to pop her cherry, but he won't touch her because of her age. When her birthday finally makes it legal, he arranges for a very special celebration.*

www.eroticawriter.net/YoungEager.html

Or visit
http://eroticawriter.net/
to find links to individual stories
and additional collections
and

For darker, edgier fiction
look for books by
KORIN DUSHAYL
**The Darker Side
of Intimacy
transgressivewriter.com**